Grolier Books

© 1992 The Walt Disney Company

No portion of this book may be reproduced
without the written consent of The Walt Disney Company.

Produced by Kroha Associates, Inc.
Middletown, Connecticut

Illustrated by Yakovetic Productions

Printed in the United States of America.
ISBN 0-7172-8388-7

Bee Nice

It was such a beautiful spring day that the birds could not keep themselves from flying just for fun, and Scuttle was no exception. He spent the morning soaring above the island enjoying the view below and the warm sun above. It made him very happy, but it made him very sleepy, too — so he decided to settle under his favorite tree for a midday nap.

What Scuttle didn't know was that — as of today — his tree had also become the favorite spot of the island's honey bees. He discovered this scary fact when, just as he was about to drift off into dreamland, a great big bee landed right on his beak!

"Go away!" Scuttle cried, swatting at the bee. But the bee didn't go away. He stung Scuttle instead. "Ow!" howled Scuttle, "that hurts!" Just then the other bees saw Scuttle, too, and soon they were all chasing him away from the tree.

When the bees had chased Scuttle far enough
from their tree, they hurried back to the hive.
Scuttle was furious! "There has to be a way
to get rid of those pesky bees so I can finish
my nap," he muttered to himself. Then he
remembered an empty pickle jar that he had
saved — he could use that to trap the bees!

Scuttle poked holes in the top of the jar with a sharp piece of shell so the bees could breathe. Then he quietly sneaked up on the hive, and placed the mouth of the jar over the opening. Scuttle gently jiggled the hive and the worried bees came zooming out, right into his jar!

"I got you!" he laughed as he quickly put the lid on the jar. But the bees were buzzing so loudly that Scuttle still couldn't sleep, so he put the jar behind a bush on the far side of the lagoon.

The evil sea witch, Ursula, saw Scuttle with the bees, and got an idea of her own. *I love honey,* she thought, *and with those bees all nicely trapped in a jar, I can have all the honey I want, whenever I want it!*

And so Ursula carried the jar of bees beneath the sea inside a magic air bubble. "Now, make me some honey!" she commanded when they arrived at her cave. But the poor bees just looked out from the jar, sad and frightened to be so far away from their home.

A few days later, while
Scales the dragon was
baking up a big batch of
seaberry muffins for his friends,
he ran out of honey. But when he went to the hive to get some more, he
discovered that the bees were gone! *No bees means no more honey!* Scales
thought to himself. *I must find out what happened to the bees!*

Scales hurried to the lagoon to tell Ariel and Sebastian the crab what he had discovered. "The bees are missing and there isn't any more honey anywhere! Will you help me find them?"

"Of course we will!" replied Sebastian, who loved to put lots and lots of honey on his seaberry muffins.

"I hope the bees are all right," Ariel said. "Let's go look for them right now!"

The three friends searched and searched, but they couldn't find the bees anywhere. What they did find was Scuttle asleep under a tree.

"Scuttle, wake up!" shouted Ariel. "We need your help!"

Scuttle awoke with a start. "Wha-what's the matter?" he asked.

"The bees are missing!" said Scales.

"No, they're not," Scuttle replied. "I put them in a jar behind that bush just the other day."

"Why would you do a silly thing like that?" Ariel asked. "Don't you know how important it is for the bees to be free?"

"But they were bothering me so much I couldn't get to sleep," replied the bird. A frustrated Sebastian explained to Scuttle how everyone needed the bees for honey, and how the bees needed pollen from the flowers to make the honey. Scuttle liked honey almost as much as Sebastian did, and so he agreed to let the bees go. But when they went to the place where he had left the jar, it was gone!

No one knew that Ursula had taken the bees. All they knew was that without bees, life on the island would never be the same. There would be no more honey for them to put on their seaberry muffins. Even worse, the flowers wouldn't be able to grow without the bees to help spread their pollen. Poor Scuttle felt terrible. He scratched his head and tried to remember, which wasn't very easy for him to do. He was sure he had left the bees behind the bush.

Meanwhile, Ursula had been trying for days to get the bees to make her some honey inside their jar, but without success. When she looked in her magic pearl and saw Ariel and her friends looking for the bees, she had an idea. *Maybe I can trick Ariel into showing me how to get the bees to make honey,* she thought.

And so, taking the bees with her, she swam to the surface.

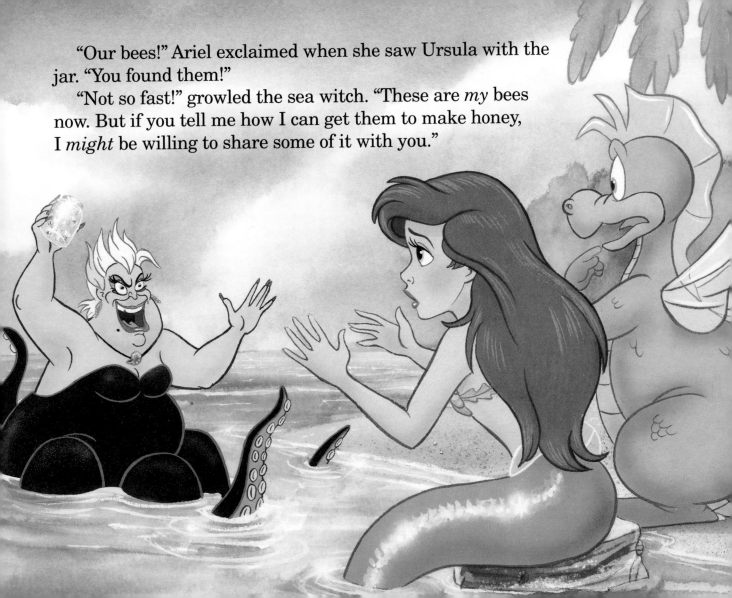

"Our bees!" Ariel exclaimed when she saw Ursula with the jar. "You found them!"

"Not so fast!" growled the sea witch. "These are *my* bees now. But if you tell me how I can get them to make honey, I *might* be willing to share some of it with you."

"That's easy!" replied Ariel. "All you have to do is let the bees out of the jar for awhile."

"That's all?" asked the sea witch.

"Yes," said Ariel. "You see, the bees need the flowers to make honey."

Ariel knew that once Ursula let the bees out of the jar she'd never get them back in, which is exactly what the Little Mermaid had in mind. Sure enough, as soon as Ursula took the lid off the jar, all the bees flew out and began chasing her around the shore of the island. "You tricked me!" the sea witch howled as she dived back under the water.

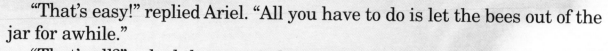

One day after the bees were back buzzing around their hive, Ariel and her friends celebrated by having a picnic. "These muffins taste so much better with yummy honey on them," Scales said.

"They certainly do!" agreed Sebastian. "I'm glad to have the bees back where they belong. It's all right to put honey in a jar, but not bees."

"I guess you're right," Scuttle said. "Everything in nature has its place — even bees!"